"I know how to love!"

Blake made the admission grudgingly, through gritted teeth. "You've taught me that."

Joy—pervasive, euphoric—sang through Jamie. She took a step toward him. "Then all we have left is the laughing. You smiled once in the rain. Maybe you can do it again. Tilt your face up to the sky—"

"Forget the damn rain." He pulled her into his arms, and on his face was a look that took the breath from her body. "I have one last question for the teacher.... What are you like to make love to, Jamie? Sweet and shy, as if it were the first time? Or passionate and hot ... as if it were the last?"

Then he kissed her as if he meant to find out.

SHIRLEY LARSON
is also the author
of this novel in
Temptation

WHERE THE HEART IS